JF WARNER
Warner, Gertrude Chandler,
1890-1979, author.
The doughnut whodunit

THE BOXCAR CHILDREN MYSTERIES

THE MYSTERY OF THE WILD PONIES
THE MYSTERY IN THE COMPUTER GAME
THE HONEYBEE MYSTERY
THE MYSTERY AT THE CROOKED HOUSE
THE HOCKEY MYSTERY
THE MYSTERY OF THE MIDNIGHT DOG
THE MYSTERY OF THE SCREECH OWL
THE SUMMER CAMP MYSTERY
THE COPYCAT MYSTERY
THE HAUNTED CLOCK TOWER MYSTERY
THE MYSTERY OF THE TIGER'S EYE
THE DISAPPEARING STAIRCASE MYSTERY
THE MYSTERY ON BLIZZARD MOUNTAIN
THE MYSTERY OF THE SPIDER'S CLUE
THE CANDY FACTORY MYSTERY
THE MYSTERY OF THE MUMMY'S CURSE
THE MYSTERY OF THE STAR RUBY
THE STUFFED BEAR MYSTERY
THE MYSTERY OF ALLIGATOR SWAMP
THE MYSTERY AT SKELETON POINT
THE TATTLETALE MYSTERY
THE COMIC BOOK MYSTERY
THE GREAT SHARK MYSTERY
THE ICE CREAM MYSTERY
THE MIDNIGHT MYSTERY
THE MYSTERY IN THE FORTUNE COOKIE
THE BLACK WIDOW SPIDER MYSTERY
THE RADIO MYSTERY
THE MYSTERY OF THE RUNAWAY GHOST
THE FINDERS KEEPERS MYSTERY
THE MYSTERY OF THE HAUNTED BOXCAR
THE CLUE IN THE CORN MAZE
THE GHOST OF THE CHATTERING BONES
THE SWORD OF THE SILVER KNIGHT
THE GAME STORE MYSTERY
THE MYSTERY OF THE ORPHAN TRAIN
THE VANISHING PASSENGER
THE GIANT YO-YO MYSTERY
THE CREATURE IN OGOPOGO LAKE
THE ROCK 'N' ROLL MYSTERY
THE SECRET OF THE MASK
THE SEATTLE PUZZLE
THE GHOST IN THE FIRST ROW
THE BOX THAT WATCH FOUND
A HORSE NAMED DRAGON

THE GREAT DETECTIVE RACE
THE GHOST AT THE DRIVE-IN MOVIE
THE MYSTERY OF THE TRAVELING TOMATOES
THE SPY GAME
THE DOG-GONE MYSTERY
THE VAMPIRE MYSTERY
SUPERSTAR WATCH
THE SPY IN THE BLEACHERS
THE AMAZING MYSTERY SHOW
THE PUMPKIN HEAD MYSTERY
THE CUPCAKE CAPER
THE CLUE IN THE RECYCLING BIN
MONKEY TROUBLE
THE ZOMBIE PROJECT
THE GREAT TURKEY HEIST
THE GARDEN THIEF
THE BOARDWALK MYSTERY
THE MYSTERY OF THE FALLEN TREASURE
THE RETURN OF THE GRAVEYARD GHOST
THE MYSTERY OF THE STOLEN SNOWBOARD
THE MYSTERY OF THE WILD WEST BANDIT
THE MYSTERY OF THE SOCCER SNITCH
THE MYSTERY OF THE GRINNING GARGOYLE
THE MYSTERY OF THE MISSING POP IDOL
THE MYSTERY OF THE STOLEN DINOSAUR BONES
THE MYSTERY AT THE CALGARY STAMPEDE
THE SLEEPY HOLLOW MYSTERY
THE LEGEND OF THE IRISH CASTLE
THE CELEBRITY CAT CAPER
HIDDEN IN THE HAUNTED SCHOOL
THE ELECTION DAY DILEMMA
JOURNEY ON A RUNAWAY TRAIN
THE CLUE IN THE PAPYRUS SCROLL
THE DETOUR OF THE ELEPHANTS
THE SHACKLETON SABOTAGE
THE KHIPU AND THE FINAL KEY
THE DOUGHNUT WHODUNIT
THE ROBOT RANSOM

THE BOXCAR CHILDREN®

CREATED BY
GERTRUDE CHANDLER WARNER

BOOK

146

THE DOUGHNUT WHODUNIT

ILLUSTRATED BY
ANTHONY VanARSDALE

Contents

Double Doughnut Trouble?

"*Brr!* It's colder than I thought," said Benny as he zipped up his jacket.

It was the first day of spring break, and Benny, Violet, Jessie, and Henry Alden were enjoying their new freedom by going on a walk through downtown Greenfield, Connecticut. The morning air was just beginning to warm.

"Aren't you glad I made you wear your coat?" Jessie asked. She was twelve and always looking out for her six-year-old brother.

"It definitely doesn't feel like summer yet, but it sure is a beautiful day," said Violet, who was ten.

All around them, the green in bushes, trees, and grass was starting to show. The sun was warming the dew off of the grass.

"Where should we go first?" asked Henry. He was fourteen and the oldest of the Alden children.

"I'd love at least one new book to read," said Jessie. "Why don't we go to the library? We could all get books."

Benny huffed. "Going to the library is almost like going to school," he said. "We just got done with school yesterday!"

Jessie smiled. "All right, Benny. What do you want to do?"

"I don't know. Something fun—and tasty!" Benny said.

Henry chuckled. "We just finished breakfast. Maybe you can wait a little while to eat."

Benny shrugged and hopped from foot to foot down the sidewalk, ahead of the others.

"What if we decorate the boxcar?" asked Violet. "It's been a long winter, and it could use some attention."

The Aldens really liked the boxcar. It had played an important part in their lives. After the children's parents died, the children had run away.

Double Doughnut Trouble?

They were afraid of their grandfather, whom they had never met. They worried he would be mean to them, so they hid in the woods, where they found the boxcar. For a while, the children lived in the boxcar. They had lots of adventures and even found their dog, Watch, in the woods. Later they learned that Grandfather was very kind and had been looking for them. He brought the Aldens and Watch to live with him, and he had the boxcar put in the backyard, to use as a clubhouse.

"Good idea, Violet," said Jessie. "Let's be on the lookout for decorating ideas for the boxcar." Jessie patted her pocket where she kept her notebook and pen. She usually took those things wherever she went.

"And I'll start thinking of projects to work on," said Henry. "I've been meaning to—"

"Woah! Look at that!" said Benny, who had stopped ahead of them. He pointed across Main Street, where people were standing in a line that stretched far down the sidewalk.

"I wonder what they're waiting for," said Jessie.

"What does the sign say?" asked Benny. "The

letters are all funny shaped. I can't read them."

Jessie read aloud from the colorful sign. "'The Donut Dispensary.' That place wasn't here the last time we came into town."

"What's a disp...a dispens...a whatever it's called?" asked Benny. "And did they spell *doughnut* wrong?"

"A dispensary's a place that gives out things to people," Jessie explained. "I don't think anyone uses that word much anymore. But a lot of people spell *doughnut d-o-n-u-t*. I think it's okay to spell it either way."

"Another doughnut shop!" said Benny. "That makes two in Greenfield!"

The Aldens crossed the street. But when they got to the store, they couldn't see very much. The crowd of people was too thick to see into the window or doorway.

"Maybe we should come back later when the line isn't so long," said Henry.

Violet agreed. "Even if people think this place is so great, I can't believe their doughnuts are better than the ones they make at Delilah's Doughnut

Shop. And there's never a line like this there."

"These doughnuts look crazy!" said Benny, coming out of the crowd. "I ducked down and got close to the window, and I saw one that had bacon and syrup on it!"

"I don't know if that sounds great or terrible." Jessie chuckled. "But I am curious what other kinds they have."

As the children watched, people strolled out of the busy doorway carrying small bags and paper coffee cups.

"It's really full in there," Henry said, standing on his tiptoes. "It doesn't look like there's any place to sit."

"That's weird," said Violet. "I like to sit down and enjoy my food, like we do at Delilah's."

"I agree," said Jessie. "Why don't we go see what's going on there?"

"And get some doughnuts!" said Benny. "Do you think they have ones with bacon and syrup?"

"Oh, Benny," said Jessie. "You know the real attraction is our friends, Dawn and Steve. I wonder how they feel about the new doughnut shop in town."

Double Doughnut Trouble?

The children turned to leave, but a tall, thin delivery man in a brown uniform was right behind them. He had a two-wheeled hand truck loaded with boxes and was trying to get through the crowd.

"Sorry, folks," he said. "Sorry. I need to get in the door. Thanks for moving aside."

As the Aldens stepped to the side, one of the boxes started to fall and Henry caught it.

"Woah, nice reflexes, young man," the delivery man said. "Thanks for the help."

"No problem," said Henry, setting the box back onto the stack. "Do you need help getting that inside?"

The delivery man shook his head. "I should be able to weave my way in. Thanks again."

As the man disappeared into the crowd, the Aldens continued on their way. It was only a few blocks to Delilah's.

When the four children stepped inside the shop, they breathed in the wonderful smell of freshly made doughnuts. There were plenty of tables in the large, open room. Customers sat, chatting and enjoying themselves. A few people stood at the counter, ordering.

"Aldens!" called a friendly voice. "How nice to see you." A short, dark-skinned woman with big, smiling eyes came around the corner, wiping her hands on her apron. She gave each of the children a quick hug.

"Hi, Dawn," said Jessie. "We came to see you and your husband."

"And your doughnuts," said Benny.

Dawn laughed. "Of course you did!" she said. "Please, take a table and come up and order what you'd like. Steve is really busy right now, but I'm sure he'll say hello when he sees you."

It looked like both Steve and Dawn were extra busy, even though the shop wasn't full of customers. The children could easily see Steve because he towered over most of the customers. He had wavy silver hair and broad shoulders. He came hurrying out from the back room with a large tray of doughnuts to put onto the racks behind the counter. Then he turned quickly to help the next customer at the counter. Dawn rang up orders, brought customers their doughnuts, and refilled coffee cups for people at tables. She barely seemed to have time to say hello to customers.

"I've never seen Dawn and Steve so busy," said Jessie. "Dawn usually loves chatting with people. Sometimes she sits right down at the table!"

"You're right, Jessie," said Henry. "I wonder what's going on."

The Aldens left their jackets at a table and went up to the counter. On the racks were signs with the names of each kind of doughnut: glazed, powdered sugar dunkers, chocolate dunkers, jelly doughnuts, and Delilah's Classic Buttermilk Dollie Doughnuts.

"They all look so good," said Jessie. "I don't think I can decide. The chocolate dunkers are kind of gooey in a great way. And the buttermilk ones are so puffy and tasty. And then there are the glazed ones that practically melt in your mouth. Mmmm."

"We could each order a different one and share them," suggested Violet.

"You guys can do that," said Benny. "I want one of each!"

Henry, Violet, and Jessie laughed. "You can order one, Benny," said Henry. "We can each pick our own favorite. And let's get some milk too."

All this time, Steve hurried to and fro, carrying trays of doughnuts from the back room. When he saw the Aldens, he smiled and waved at them, and then he hurried away.

"Poor Steve," said Dawn, after she took the children's orders. "Our apprentice baker quit last week, and we don't have a replacement yet. We have more work than we can keep up with right now."

"What's an apprentice?" asked Violet.

"It's someone who's training for a job," said Dawn. "Nathan had been with us for a year. He was really getting to know the business."

"Why did he quit?" asked Benny. "I think it would be fun to work here."

Dawn sighed and looked down. "I wish I knew why he quit. Nathan was such a good worker, even though he and Steve sometimes disagreed. He told us he was leaving only three days before he went. That's not enough time to find a good replacement." Dawn looked frustrated and a little sad.

"We can help, Dawn," offered Henry. "We're on spring break now. We can do lots of things for you this week." The other children nodded.

"That would be such a big help!" said Dawn. "But are you kids sure you want to be helping out here while you're on break?"

"What could be better than being surrounded by doughnuts?" asked Benny.

Dawn broke into a smile. "Let me think of some jobs that you children could help me with, and you can get started tomorrow."

"We can help you with that too," said Jessie, pulling out her notebook and pencil. "I'll make a list of the jobs you want us to do."

"Great!" said Dawn. "But first, have your doughnuts. I'll come over to your table when things quiet down."

While they waited, the children ate their doughnuts and looked around the familiar shop. The walls were covered with old-fashioned, tan wallpaper that had tiny, pale flowers on it. There were knickknacks on shelves and hanging black-and-white photographs from old times. Brown ruffled curtains hung from the middle to the bottom of each window. The floor was made of dark, square tiles. The tables, chairs, and even the counter where the doughnuts were sold were all made of dark, smooth wood.

"This shop feels happy," said Benny as he wiped crumbs from his mouth.

Henry laughed. "I think you mean that you feel happy being here, Benny," he said.

"Delilah's has lots of happy customers," said Jessie. "Most of them stay and chat with each other."

"I like hanging out here too. The old photos and posters are so interesting," said Violet. "They seem like old friends I'm visiting."

On the wall were photos of Steve's parents, Delilah and Fred, who had opened the shop many years before. There were also old photos of the shop itself. One of them showed the huge neon sign that had once been outside.

The posters were very old advertisements with drawings of smiling soldiers. Young women offered the soldiers doughnuts from huge tubs. Some posters mentioned National Doughnut Day. Others had photos of women called "Doughnut Girls."

Double Doughnut Trouble?

Dawn was just passing by with her coffeepot. "Have you seen the new doughnut shop yet? My friend Hilda Ramirez is the owner."

"Your friend owns The Donut Dispensary?" asked Henry. "Aren't you worried that her store will take away your customers?"

"I don't think that will happen," said Dawn. "Our shops are different in many ways. I think Hilda will find her own customers. Besides, people who come to Delilah's are very loyal. We always have the same five favorite doughnuts and the best coffee in town. More important, we give them a lot more than just doughnuts and coffee."

Dawn's big, warm smile got even bigger.

"What do you mean more than doughnuts and coffee?" asked Violet.

"You know," said Henry. "Like Benny's happy feeling. Right, Dawn?"

"Exactly!" said Dawn.

The door banged open. "Oh! It's Charlie," she said. "I have to go." Dawn hurried to help hold open the door.

"That's the same delivery man we saw at The

Donut Dispensary," whispered Henry.

The tall, thin man in the brown uniform frowned as he wheeled his hand truck through the door. He seemed to be complaining to Dawn, who was helping him. The hand truck banged into Jessie's chair, and the delivery man swerved to avoid hitting Benny in the leg. The children heard the man grumble, "If you'd just clear a path to the back instead of having all these tables here, I wouldn't have so much trouble getting my hand truck through the room!"

The Aldens watched the man push his hand truck toward the back room.

"That was strange," said Jessie. "That man seemed so nice when we saw him at the other doughnut shop."

"He was nice," said Henry. "But not now. Not here."

Stranger with a Rolling Pin

The next morning, the children headed toward Delilah's at seven o'clock. They had decided to get up extra early so they could start helping as soon as possible.

Main Street was quiet, and most of the shops weren't yet open. So the Aldens were surprised when they got to Delilah's and the lights were on and the OPEN sign hung in the window. Inside, no customers were there yet, but the smell of baking doughnuts wafted from the back room.

Bells on the door jingled as it closed behind the children, and within seconds, Steve emerged from the back.

"Wow," said Benny. "You get up early!"

The Doughnut Whodunit

"That's what bakers do," said Steve, grinning. "Come on back to the kitchen and I'll show you." The Aldens followed him behind the counter and into the baking area, where Dawn had an apron on and was rolling some dough.

"Doughnuts take a lot of time to make," Steve said as he laid out a batch of just-fried doughnuts on a tray. "We start the night before."

"I've made cookies and cake," said Jessie. "But you don't need hours and hours to make those."

"Doughnuts have yeast in them," Steve explained. "We have to give them lots of time to let the yeast do its work, so the dough sits overnight. We fry the doughnuts the next morning. The ones that need icing have to cool for a while too, before we finish them. And our first customers will be here around eight o'clock."

"That's a lot of work," said Henry. "What can we do to help you?"

"Jessie," said Dawn, as she looked in from the doorway, "why don't you get out the list of jobs we made yesterday?"

Dawn and the Aldens went to the front of the

shop. Jessie pulled out her notebook. "I put a name next to each job so we know exactly what to do," she said. "It's all organized."

Jessie read from her list. "Violet, Steve can show you and me how to arrange the doughnuts on trays and how to put icing on the chocolate ones. Henry can carry the trays from the baking area and put them on the racks in the front of the shop. And Dawn is going to show Henry how to take orders from customers and how to run the cash register."

"What can I do?" asked Benny.

"You have a fun job," Jessie told Benny. "Henry will tell you which doughnuts people order. You can put them on plates or in bags to give to customers."

"I like that job!" said Benny.

"This is a big help," said Dawn. "Steve and I can manage the rest of the work more easily when each of you does your part." Dawn looked at Jessie again. "What about the last job?"

"You'll need all of us for that," said Jessie. The other Aldens crowded around her to find out what the job was.

"Delilah's needs redecorating," said Jessie.

"We're going to help make a plan with Dawn and Steve. If there's time this week, we can paint and do other things to make the shop look brighter and more fun."

"We'd like to keep our tables and chairs, and of course the counter. We're just thinking about repainting the walls, and maybe replacing those curtains." Dawn waved her arm toward the windows.

"Please keep the photos and the posters forever," said Violet.

"Absolutely!" said Dawn. "Now, let's get to work."

Everyone worked hard all morning. Delilah's had plenty of customers. In the kitchen, Jessie and Violet set up clean trays, placed the doughnuts in rows, and added the icing to the doughnuts. This last part was a messy, sticky job until the girls got the hang of it. Henry helped Steve bring in the finished trays of doughnuts and made sure the labels with their names were correct. He also got his own order pad for writing down what people wanted. Dawn complimented Henry on his friendly service to customers.

Benny was happy when he was busy—and he

was busy! Dawn made sure he scrubbed his hands, and then Benny took over serving customers. He placed each doughnut on a small, white plate and carefully walked the order to the person who sat waiting for it. Then he would race back to get the next order. Dawn took care of milk and coffee that people wanted. Benny also put doughnuts in white paper bags, making sure the doughnuts didn't get mashed or crumbled.

Around lunchtime, most customers were gone. The doughnut racks were full, waiting for the late-afternoon crowd. Steve hung up his apron. He and the children sat down at a table for a much-needed break and some lunch.

"I'm glad you're all here today," Steve said, smiling. "I'm making a very special kind of doughnut. Once in a while I like to change up the menu, just a little bit."

"What kind of doughnut is it?" asked Benny.

"It was one of my mother's very favorites, from a secret recipe my dad developed after World War II. I'm the only person who knows how to make it."

"What makes it special?" Violet asked.

Steve opened his eyes wide and whispered, "It's made from potatoes! We call it The Masher."

"Potatoes!" said Jessie. "I've never heard of doughnuts made out of potatoes. That sounds weird. Sorry!"

"That's perfectly okay, Jessie. Some people really love The Masher," Steve said. "But not everyone. I make them only in small batches—and not very often either. Come on." He stood up. "I'll show you what they look like. They're tricky to make because the dough has an unusual texture. There's a special way that I cut them out too. And they're kind of difficult to fry."

"They're square!" said Violet when they were all in the kitchen. "How did you do that?"

Steve laughed. "That's the easy part. And it's not a family secret."

Steve showed the children a special cutter for making square doughnuts. "We still give them round holes," he said.

"It smells familiar in here. Sort of like dinner... like mashed potatoes," said Henry.

"That's right, Henry," said Steve. "You have a

very good nose."

Steve took his jacket down from a hook on the wall. "These doughnuts still need to rise for a while," he said. "Now that it's quieted down, Dawn and I need to run some important errands. We've been so busy this week, we could hardly leave the store. Do you think the four of you could keep an eye on things while we're gone?"

Jessie nodded. "We've learned a lot this morning. We can do it. Because we have plenty of doughnuts ready, Violet and I can help Henry and Benny."

"That's great!" said Dawn, coming into the kitchen. "I'll just get my coat, and we'll be on our way. We'll be gone for a couple of hours."

"Can I have a doughnut while you're gone?" asked Benny. "I'll work extra hard."

Dawn laughed and she put on her hat. "You can pick out whichever one you want, Benny. You're my chief server, after all."

It didn't take long before the children got busy again. Customers came in wanting doughnuts to go and doughnuts with coffee. Henry even took phone orders, writing on his notepad by the cash register. Benny scooped up doughnuts and put them on plates and in bags. Violet and Jessie served drinks and cleaned up tables when customers left.

Jessie was clearing a table when the bells on the door gave a jingle. She noticed a young man with curly red hair and freckles looking around the shop. He didn't seem to want to buy anything—he just stood near the door. Then he turned and walked straight into the back room.

Who is that strange man? Jessie wondered. She followed him into the back.

At first, she couldn't see anyone, but then she heard some shuffling and banging. Jessie looked around the big work table. The man was on his hands and knees, moving some boxes around and digging through them.

"Hello?" said Jessie loudly. "Can I help you?"

The young man jumped up, holding on to a rolling pin. Jessie took a step backward.

"Oh!" said the man. "I thought I was here alone. I...I was looking for my rolling pin. I left it here last week." He blushed red.

"Are you Nathan?" asked Jessie. The man nodded.

"So...you found your rolling pin?"

"Yes. I'm really glad," said Nathan. "I'm going to need it right away—at the other doughnut shop. I work there now." He put the rolling pin into his backpack, hurried out of the back room, and left the shop.

A little while later, Dawn and Steve came back, carrying a few packages.

"We served eighteen customers," Benny told them. "And we sold thirty-three doughnuts, nine cups of coffee, and four glasses of milk. We were busy!"

"Well done!" said Steve. "Now I'd better get busy putting this extra butter in the freezer." Steve hurried to the back room.

"We have a surprise for each of you," said Dawn, reaching into a shopping bag. Dawn pulled out four bright blue aprons in different sizes. They were the same style as the ones Dawn and Steve wore. A loop at the top went over the person's head, and the apron covered them from neck to knees and tied in the back.

"These are for my favorite assistants," she said. The children tried on their aprons.

"Wow!" said Benny. "I'm a real doughnut shop helper now." He gave Dawn and Steve his biggest grin.

"I love these," Violet told Dawn. "They're such a beautiful color. Thank you so much. I'm bringing my camera tomorrow so we can take our picture wearing our new aprons."

"You didn't have to think of us, Dawn," said Henry. "You have enough to think about now."

"Speaking of which..." Jessie hesitated. "Something happened while you were gone. Something strange."

"What happened?" Dawn asked.

"Nathan was here. I followed him into the back room," said Jessie. "He went in there without telling us. I thought maybe he was avoiding us."

"Oh?" said Dawn. "Why on Earth would he want to avoid you?"

Jessie shrugged. "He said he came for his rolling pin."

"Ah, yes," said Dawn, nodding. "Nathan did leave his rolling pin here last week."

"But why would he go straight to the back room

without talking to any of us?" asked Henry.

"I don't know," Dawn replied. "Maybe he was embarrassed about quitting so suddenly." Dawn sat down at a table and continued. "Nathan was often unhappy about things at Delilah's."

"Unhappy?" said Violet. "But this is such a great place to be."

"Well, not so much for Nathan, it seems," said Dawn. "He had trouble remembering the recipes and techniques that we use. And Steve wouldn't let Nathan write anything down while he was learning."

"Why did Steve stop Nathan from writing things down?" asked Henry. "Isn't that a good thing, like taking notes in school?"

Dawn explained. "Steve's recipes come from his parents. Steve memorized them all, and he didn't want anyone to write them down. That way, no one could copy them."

"You mean steal them? Who would want to steal a recipe?" asked Benny.

"Another doughnut shop might," said Violet.

"Oh!" said Jessie. "I almost forgot. Nathan said he's going to work for The Donut Dispensary."

Dawn's smile faded and she sighed. "Steve and I really like Nathan. I'm sure he would have gotten the hang of things here. I think Nathan really did enjoy the business." Dawn shook her head. "I wish he hadn't quit. We were hoping he could take over Delilah's when we retire someday."

"And now that Nathan's working for the other shop, I guess he'll never take over Delilah's," said Henry.

"No," said Dawn. "It doesn't seem that way. Nathan will be so hard to replace. We need a reliable worker who can learn from us. We also need someone who's interested in staying with our business for a long time."

"We'll keep helping you this week, Dawn," said Henry. "And we can come on the weekends when we go back to school. You'll find a new apprentice soon."

"Thanks again, all of you," said Dawn. "You've come at just the right time. You've done a great job so far, and there's more to do today. In fact, soon it'll be time to close up for the day. We need to show you how it's done."

The Aldens helped close up the shop. They

bagged unsold doughnuts to give to a homeless shelter. Then they wiped down the countertops and washed the floors. Steve stayed in the back, making up the next day's doughs, which had to rise overnight. Henry helped Dawn tally up the day's receipts.

Benny looked at the doughnut racks. "Now all we have left are The Mashers—one dozen of them," he said.

"They'll still be fresh for tomorrow," said Steve, "because we made them late in the day."

CHAPTER

Closed!

When the Aldens arrived at Delilah's the next morning, the lights were on in the shop as usual. But the sign on the door said CLOSED, and the door was locked.

"That's strange," said Jessie. "The shop is usually open by now."

"Maybe Dawn and Steve woke up late," said Benny.

Henry tapped on the glass, and after a moment, Steve came to the door.

"Hi, helpers. You can come in," he said. "But we won't open till the afternoon."

"Why aren't you open this morning?" asked Henry. "Did something happen?"

The Doughnut Whodunit

Steve ran his hands through his hair. "Someone broke into the shop last night."

"Oh no!" said Jessie. "Was anything taken?"

"We don't think so," said Steve, "but we're still figuring out if anything is missing. Nothing of value is gone—no money or special equipment. A lot of things have been moved around, though."

After they were all inside, Steve locked the door. The children looked around the shop. Photos and posters had been taken down and now lay on the floor. Behind the counter, the cash register sat on its side. Notepads, pens, and receipts were all jumbled up on the floor. In the back room, boxes had been pulled out. Utensils, spices, and bags of ingredients were shifted out of place.

Jessie pulled out her notebook and took notes about the changes.

"Who would have done this?" Violet asked.

"I've got a pretty good idea," said Steve as he started walking around the kitchen, picking up things and putting them where they belonged.

"Do you think it was Nathan?" asked Henry.

"Whoever got in here last night didn't break the

lock," Steve said. "Nathan had a key to the shop when he worked here. He could have made a copy before he gave the original one back to me."

"Nathan was here yesterday," said Jessie. "He got his rolling pin. Why would he want to break into the shop after that?"

Steve just shook his head without answering. "Maybe he didn't find what he was really looking for."

Everyone gathered at a table in the front of the shop.

"Does anyone else have a copy of your key?" asked Henry.

"Charlie, the delivery man has one," said Dawn, who was picking up decorations that had fallen to the floor.

Steve stood up again and started pacing. "Charlie would never do anything like this," he said. "We've known him..." He trailed off. "We've known him for a very long time."

"Charlie isn't all that nice," said Violet. "Remember? He came here to deliver things yesterday. He was rude to Dawn."

"He can be cranky, Violet," said Dawn. "But Charlie is someone we trust. Besides, he has no reason to come into the shop without our being here."

"Hey!" Benny suddenly shouted. "I know what's missing—The Mashers! There were twelve of them last night. I remember—I counted them. Now they're gone."

It was true. Steve and Henry had carefully wrapped the tray of remaining Mashers the night before. Now, the tray was there, but it was empty.

"Oh no!" said Violet. "If someone took The Mashers, maybe they took the secret recipe too."

Steve gave a laugh that sounded a little like a bark. "That's something no one can do, Violet. My recipes are safely locked up—in here." Steve tapped his head. "They aren't written down anywhere."

"Well," said Dawn. "We won't get this place ready for customers by sitting around talking. Steve, why don't you take the boys into the kitchen? Violet, Jessie, and I can clean up the front."

"I have an idea," said Violet. "We're going to paint the walls anyway. Why don't we wait to put the pictures back? At least that will save us some time when we start to paint."

"Good idea," said Dawn. "I'll get some boxes. You and Jessie can help me stack the pictures and take the boxes into the storeroom. And then you can start planning the redecoration project."

Violet and Jessie smiled. "We like decorating, but we don't have any ideas yet," said Violet. "Dawn, do you?"

"The wallpaper will have to go," said Dawn. "That's all I know so far. What if you girls check out the decor in The Donut Dispensary? You might get some ideas there. Hilda is very creative."

"Will your friend mind if we check out her shop?" asked Violet.

Dawn shook her head. "We like sharing our knowledge. It helps us both." Dawn smiled. "As a matter of fact, Hilda helped me out when we first met. I told her I wanted to learn Spanish. So, she and I bartered. She gave me Spanish lessons, and I gave her business advice to help her get started."

"So, that's what bartering means? You trade help?" asked Violet.

"People trade help or ideas or things," said

Dawn. "Just not money."

"But you didn't trade your recipes with her, right?" asked Jessie.

"No, not our recipes," said Dawn. "Some of those have been in Steve's family since the 1940s. He wants to keep those private."

While the others stayed at Delilah's to clean up, Jessie and Violet headed to The Donut Dispensary.

"I just wish bad things hadn't happened to Delilah's," Jessie said.

"Well, at least we can help out by decorating," said Violet. "I brought my camera in case we see things we like."

Then a worried look crossed Violet's face. As she walked along, she asked her sister, "If stealing someone's recipe is bad, isn't it bad to steal ideas for decorating?"

"I don't think so," said Jessie. "We don't want to make Delilah's look exactly like The Donut Dispensary, anyway. We're going to come up with our own ideas."

"Okay," said Violet slowly. "I know I can get my own ideas for things. But maybe we should buy doughnuts when we get there."

"Sure," said Jessie. "I don't want to go there and just look either."

"Dawn and Hilda are friends," said Violet. "So, it's okay to look and take pictures. But I'm curious about these doughnuts!"

There was no line outside The Donut Dispensary that day, but inside it was busy. While Jessie and Violet waited in line to order, Jessie wrote in her notebook and Violet took photos. It was a very small shop, big enough for people to stand in, but not big enough for tables. Everything was colored bright white and emergency orange. There were a few shiny stools with orange seats on them. From the ceiling hung sleek, shiny metal lights. A huge metal sign along one wall spelled out DONUTS. Loud music played through speakers.

"I feel like I'm in a space ship," said Violet. "Maybe it's heading toward the sun."

"It's *way* bright in here," said Jessie. "The music makes me feel like dancing." She closed her eyes and made tiny jumps in place.

When they reached the counter area, the girls

looked at the doughnuts lined up under a glass case. Some of them had funny names, like The Frida Kahlo, The Tsunami, and Custer's Last Stand. Some were huge, with masses of filling spilling out and things like jelly beans and crumbled bacon on top. Others were plainer looking but had bizarre ingredients like kale, jalapeno peppers, or green tea.

"I'm going to get one of those twisty ones with the purple designs on it," said Violet. "The sign says there's a surprise inside them."

"I think I'll get a Triple Mexican Chocolate Donut," said Jessie. "Maybe we should get two of each so Henry and Benny can have one also."

When it was their turn, a woman with long, black hair pulled back in a braid took their order. She had earrings on her ears, in her nose, and in one eyebrow. A butterfly tattoo sat on her upper arm. She smiled at the girls as she took their money. Her eyes were dark and friendly.

"I think you'll love those Twisters," she said. "They're our newest addition, and they're a really big seller!"

"Excuse me," said Jessie. "Are you Hilda? I'm

Closed!

Jessie, and this is my sister, Violet. We're helping Dawn at her shop."

The woman's smile got bigger. "Yes, I'm Hilda," she said. "It's so nice to meet friends of Dawn. How is everything at Delilah's? I've been meaning to stop in, but we've been very busy here."

"There's been some trouble, actually," said Jessie.

"Really?" said Hilda, looking worried. "Can you wait around for just a minute? I want to come out and talk to you."

The girls nodded.

Hilda called to a young man with a ponytail and a beard. She asked him to take over the cash register. Then she came over to the front window, where Jessie and Violet were waiting.

"What's happened?" asked Hilda.

Jessie and Violet explained about the break-in.

Hilda shook her head. "That's really a shame," she said. "I hope Dawn and Steve can reopen right away. I wish I could help somehow. Dawn was such a big help to me when I was getting started."

"If you want, we can tell Dawn you're sorry about the break-in," said Jessie. Violet nodded.

"Thanks," said Hilda. "Tell her I'll give her a call after we close up tonight."

***

When the girls got back to Delilah's, they sat down with the doughnuts.

"What are those funny looking ones?" asked Benny. "They look like number eights with purple spirals of frosting."

Closed!

"I think they're called Twisters," said Violet. "I like the shape and the twisty purple things on the icing. I picked out one of those for me and one for you, Benny. I thought you'd like them."

"What did you say?" asked Steve. He came over and stared at the doughnuts. "Where did you get these?"

"We're sorry," said Violet. "We had to buy some doughnuts at The Donut Dispensary. We felt bad about going there to just look around."

Steve ran his hands through his hair and sat down. "I don't mind that," he said. "What bothers me is that doughnut's name. And how it looks." He peered at The Twisters.

"Why does that bother you?" asked Henry.

"The Twisters look just like a Delilah's doughnut we sometimes make. It's called The Twisty."

"The sign in the other shop said The Twister has a surprise inside," said Violet.

"So does The Twisty," said Steve.

CHAPTER 4

Doughnuts for the Troops

"How strange!" said Dawn, looking down at The Twisters. "We should all take a taste of those. Do you mind sharing?"

"No," said Violet.

"I don't mind either," said Benny. "But why should we all taste them?"

"As a test," said Steve. He rubbed his chin. "I have an idea," he told the others. "I've got more dough to fry. We need to make doughnuts so we can open the shop...I think I'll make some Twisties right now. Then we can taste them both at the same time and find out if The Twister and The Twisty use the same recipe."

As usual, Steve had made batches of doughnut

dough the day before. He had taken out the dough earlier that morning and continued to let it rise. When it was time, the children helped him cut and shape the twists from loops of dough. Then they watched as Steve fried the twists.

While the doughnuts were cooling, they all sat down in the front of the shop and had sandwiches brought from home.

"I still can't understand how a Twister can be the exact same thing as a Twisty," said Violet. "Your recipes are secret!"

Steve shook his head. "I don't get it either," he said. "But we'll soon find out if they taste the same."

Benny munched on his sandwich. "How did all those doughnut ideas come from your head?" he asked Steve. "Do you have an extra big brain?"

Steve smiled. "I don't think so, Benny," he said. "I am good at memorizing things, though. Also, I spent a long time working in this shop with my mom and dad. After a while, I knew their recipes by heart."

"That's lucky," said Benny. "These are the best doughnuts ever."

The Doughnut Whodunit

"Did your parents always have a doughnut shop?" asked Henry.

"That's a good question, Henry," said Steve. "The answer is part of a story." Steve settled back in his chair. "Did you know that doughnuts were served to American soldiers all the way back in the First World War, at the beginning of the twentieth century?"

The Aldens shook their heads.

"It was a way to help make the soldiers feel good while they were far away from home."

"That's what the posters are about—the ones showing women giving soldiers doughnuts!" said Violet.

"Yes, it is," said Steve. "When World War II came along in the 1940s, my mother, Delilah, was one of the young women who went overseas to hand out doughnuts to the soldiers. That's when she met my dad, in fact. When the war ended, they came home and got married. They decided to open up a shop that would offer everybody the same kind of comfort and home-like feelings."

"So, how did your parents come up with their own recipes?" Jessie asked.

Doughnuts for the Troops

"They experimented," said Steve. "My mother liked classic recipes, like the basic cake doughnut. She made simple variations, like adding buttermilk to a recipe instead of plain milk. My dad liked to make bigger—and wackier—changes. For instance, he figured out how to use mashed potatoes to make a potato-based doughnut."

"Mashers!" said Benny.

"Right," said Steve. "My dad also tried out different shapes for doughnuts, different ingredients for icings and fillings, and wild combinations. Some of his ideas worked, and some didn't. But he never stopped experimenting."

"Well, I'm glad he kept going," said Jessie. "So... was The Twisty one of your father's ideas? It doesn't look like any other doughnut I've seen—except The Twister, of course."

"You're right about that," said Steve. "And I'm glad I kept his recipes locked up." Steve patted his head. "My dad never wrote them down. He thought someone might take advantage of his hard work."

"By stealing, right?" asked Violet.

Steve nodded. "That's what makes this copycat

doughnut so odd. I'm the only person who knows how to make them."

"What about your mother's recipes?" asked Henry. "Are they secret too?"

"Not really," said Steve. "They're classic, so most people make them pretty much the same way. I prefer making my mom's recipes. They're the ones that got this shop started. They're the most like the ones the soldiers had. I believe there are important reasons to carry on what my parents started. I want to keep Delilah's traditions going as long as I can."

"I feel like I saw a picture of your family somewhere," said Violet.

"Yes," said Steve. "There's one in the hallway back by the storage room. I think it's still hanging up."

Violet went to the hallway and came back with a small framed black-and-white photo. It showed a family, posing happily in front of Delilah's. The photo had been clipped from a newspaper.

"You were really young then," said Henry. "And so was the store. It doesn't look like that now."

"I was in my twenties," said Steve. "The store's been remodeled at least once since then, inside and out."

Doughnuts for the Troops

"Who's that boy?" asked Violet. She pointed to a boy in the photo about her own age.

"That's, uh, that's my brother," Steve said. He looked down at his hands.

"I didn't know you had a brother," said Violet. "What's his name? Does he live here in Greenfield?"

Steve didn't answer her. "The doughnuts should be cooled off by now," he said. "We need to put on the icing." He stood and walked quickly away from the table.

The Aldens exchanged glances.

"Am I wrong, or did it seem like Steve didn't want to talk about his brother?" asked Jessie.

Henry shrugged. "It did seem that way. But maybe he just needed to get back to the doughnuts."

"Listen to this," said Violet. She slowly read the caption at the bottom of the photo. "'The Berg family, in front of Greenfield's favorite hangout, Delilah's Doughnut Shop. Pictured: Fred and Delilah Berg with their sons, David C. and Steven F.'"

The Aldens looked at the photo again.

"So, now we know Steve's brother is named David," said Henry. "But that's all we know about him."

The Doughnut Whodunit

"Except that Steve might not want to talk about him," whispered Jessie.

When the doughnuts were cooled and Steve had added the "surprise" to each one, the children helped put icing on the batch of Twisties. They carefully added the extra designs with purple icing. Benny brought a fresh Twisty to a table out front.

"We have tests in school," he said. "But ours are never this much fun."

"It's a shame," said Henry. "I think we'll only get doughnut-tasting tests when we're on vacation."

"Unless we go to doughnut school!" said Benny. "We could experiment, like Steve's dad!"

"Right," said Henry, chuckling.

"These two doughnuts from the two different shops look almost the same," said Violet. "Even the twist designs look like copies of each other."

Steve had put a fresh Twisty on a plate. The two Twisters were on a separate plate. He cut up The Twister and one of The Twisties into pieces so everyone could have a bite of each doughnut. He kept the other Twister uncut so they could all see what it looked like.

Doughnuts for the Troops

"Now comes the best part—tasting them!" said Benny.

Dawn, Steve, and the Aldens each took a piece of both doughnuts. They carefully chewed their pieces.

"What do you think?" Steve asked.

They all agreed: the doughnuts were the same, even down to the surprise, a small amount of cinnamon-spiced apricot filling right where the doughnut loops crossed in the middle.

Dawn looked worried. "I just can't believe Hilda would try to get customers by using our recipes!" she said. "I always thought our shops would be so different that it wouldn't matter. But if our menus start to look the same, we could lose customers to the Dispensary."

"I still don't get how anyone could copy your doughnut recipe," said Jessie. "There are no recipes written down."

"What about Nathan?" suggested Henry. "He helped you make doughnuts for a year. Do you think he could have learned all the measurements and directions?"

Steve shook his head. "He's the only person I can think of who might know my recipes. But Nathan always had trouble remembering them. And it's been a while since I've made Twisties."

"Whoever copied our doughnuts didn't change their name very much," said Dawn.

"Maybe they thought no one would notice," said Jessie. "But *we* noticed."

Things were becoming more mysterious.

Where Is the Proof?

Someone knocked loudly on the shop's front door.

Dawn got up. "I thought we still had the CLOSED sign up," she said. But she opened the door to see who was there.

Charlie, the delivery man, came inside. He had a few boxes on his hand truck.

"I heard you had some trouble here," he said quietly. "I came to help."

"We don't need any help," Steve called out. "We're doing fine."

Charlie looked down. "Okay, I'll just drop off this delivery then." He started toward the back room, but as he passed them, he stopped.

"What's wrong?" asked Steve.

Where Is the Proof?

"Nothing," said Charlie, looking around the room. "I just didn't expect things to be so messed up after the break-in. I'm sorry that it happened." He headed off toward the back.

"Time to start frying dough," said Steve, standing up. "This mystery will have to wait."

They heard a loud bang from the back room.

"Sorry!" called Charlie. He appeared in a moment, holding a large, empty potato sack.

"I'll take this to the dumpster for you," he said. "It was on the floor. My hand truck got tangled up in it and bumped into a shelf."

"Thanks, Charlie," said Dawn. "Sorry it tripped up your hand truck. It shouldn't have been on the floor."

Henry held the door open for Charlie. "I was wondering," he asked Charlie, "how did you find out about the break-in so fast?"

Charlie shrugged. "This is a small town, and word travels fast," he said. "I heard Hilda and a man with a beard talking about it over at The Donut Dispensary. I made my delivery there before I came here."

Where Is the Proof?

"Well, you can tell everyone that Delilah's probably opening later today," Henry said. He watched from the doorway as Charlie put his hand truck in the back of the delivery van. But instead of taking the potato sack to the dumpster, Charlie took it with him when he got into the van.

Why didn't Charlie throw out the sack? Henry wondered.

***

The weather had turned overcast and chilly by the next morning. Gusts of dark clouds blew across a light-gray sky. The Aldens wore their rain ponchos over their warm jackets, just in case.

As they walked down Main Street toward Delilah's, they stopped to see how The Donut Dispensary was doing. The shop had just opened for the day. Already, there was a short line out front.

"I'm glad this shop is doing well," said Violet. "I think Hilda's nice. I just wish she'd stop selling copies of The Twisty."

"Look at the new sign on the window," said Benny. He read it out loud. "'Coming Soon! The Mashup—Our New Potato Donut!'"

The Doughnut Whodunit

"That sounds familiar," said Jessie. "I wonder what that Mashup looks like."

"Look at this sign," said Violet. She pointed to a chalkboard shaped like a tent on the sidewalk. "The new doughnut is square, just like a Masher!"

"This is really odd," said Henry. "First there's the copycat Twisty, and now it's a Masher. I wonder if they have paper menus inside. We could get one to show to Steve and Dawn. They might recognize the names of other copied doughnuts."

Everyone agreed. Henry stepped around the line and came back out with a paper menu.

Down the street, Delilah's was open again, with the usual morning crowd having doughnuts and coffee.

"I'm glad you're all here to help," Dawn told the Aldens after ringing up a customer. "It's been busy!"

"We have something we picked up for you and Steve," said Jessie. "It might be important."

"Okay," said Dawn. "Do you mind asking Steve if he needs help in the kitchen first?"

The Aldens pitched in during the morning rush.

Where Is the Proof?

At last, when it got quiet, Steve, Dawn, and the children all sat down with the menu from The Donut Dispensary. Jessie pulled out her notebook and pencil.

Steve scratched his head as he read. "Potato doughnuts," he muttered. "*Square* potato doughnuts, called Mashups. This just gets more and more troubling!"

"Maybe Hilda tried your doughnuts and made up her own recipe," suggested Violet. "That's not really stealing, is it?"

"No, that wouldn't be stealing," Steve said. "But I don't think that's what's going on here. This doughnut has the same ingredients! My parents worked for months to get The Masher to come out correctly. They tried and failed a lot of times until they got it right. It's a difficult recipe to make. It would be impossible to copy a Masher just by tasting one."

Dawn looked at the menu. "There are The Twisters," she said. "I wonder what 'Soldier's Specials' are. We have Special Soldier's Doughnuts for Armed Forces Day, Memorial Day, and July

Fourth. They're a kind of jelly doughnut. We fill them with raspberry jelly, cover them with powdered sugar, and put blueberries on top."

"Are any of those days coming up?" Benny licked his lips.

"You'll have to wait until a little later this spring, Benny," said Jessie.

Dawn sighed. "But if The Donut Dispensary offers them all the time, we'll have to think of a different doughnut to offer."

Steve picked up the menu. "So, that makes three doughnuts that are like the ones my parents made. All three have similar names to ours. And at least one is a definite copy. Who can be doing this—and why?" He sounded really worried.

"Why don't we talk to Melinda?" asked Dawn. "She just came in for her coffee." Dawn waved to a police officer who had walked into the shop. In the meantime, Steve went back to the counter to help customers.

Dawn got the officer a cup of coffee and brought her to the table.

"Officer Washington, these are my assistants,

the Aldens," said Dawn. "We're wondering if you could help us out with something."

"It's nice to meet you, Officer," said Henry. "Some weird things are going on. They might be coincidences, but we don't think so."

"I heard about the break-in," said Officer Washington. "Does this have anything to do with that?"

"We're not sure," said Jessie.

"What was taken in the break-in?" asked the officer.

"Some doughnuts," said Benny. "Special ones."

"Just doughnuts?" the officer asked.

"That may not sound very important," said Dawn. "But there's more to the story."

Steve returned from helping customers. "We think someone's stealing our recipes, Melinda," he said. "Several kinds of Delilah's doughnuts were copied by the new doughnut shop. Even their names are practically the same."

"So, your recipes were taken, then?" asked the officer.

"That's the oddest part," said Steve. "No one

could have taken the recipes. They've never been written down, so there aren't any copies of them."

"So, let me get this straight," said Officer Washington, "you can't show that you're missing copies of the recipes, and you can't prove the recipes were taken. I'm sorry, but I don't think there's anything that can be done."

"I see what you mean," said Steve, rubbing his chin. "I just don't know how anyone else could have those recipes."

"I wish I could help," said Officer Washington. "Please get in touch with me if you learn anything more."

After the officer left, Steve and Dawn went back to helping customers.

"It looks like we're going to need to solve this mystery ourselves," said Henry.

"I think you're right, Henry," said Jessie. "And we might save Delilah's in the process."

CHAPTER 6

Suspects

The afternoon had turned sunny and warm. The Alden children decided to eat lunch on a wooden bench in front of the store. The Aldens unzipped their jackets, and Jessie handed out sandwiches from home. The children ate quietly, enjoying the sunshine.

"I wish we could have more warm days for the rest of our spring break," said Violet. "This weather makes me feel good."

"This weather helps me think," said Henry. "And we've got a lot to think about."

As soon as Jessie finished her sandwich, she got out her notebook and pencil. "I made up a list of people who might be copying the recipes," she said. "We need to figure out who's doing that. And also, who might have broken into the shop. It could be the same person, or it might be someone else. The first person on my list is Nathan, Steve and Dawn's apprentice."

Henry crumpled up his sandwich wrappers. Benny threw his into the nearby trash can and then decided to run in circles around the bin.

"Nathan sounds like a good person to have on the list," Henry said. "He watched Steve make his recipes. He might remember them."

"But Dawn did say Nathan was bad at remembering the recipes," said Violet. "Steve wouldn't let him write them down."

"And Steve said it had been a while since he had made The Twisties," said Jessie. "Nathan would have to have planned taking the recipes for a long time."

Benny stopped running. "What if he wrote the recipes down in secret?" he asked.

The other children thought about that. Benny started running again.

Violet said, "Nathan might have taken notes and

then hidden them somewhere in the bakery."

"He could have been looking for them that time I surprised him in the back room," said Jessie. "He said he came to get his rolling pin, but what if he was looking for his notes?"

Violet said, "What if you stopped Nathan before he found the notes? That would explain why he had to break into the shop that night!"

Henry nodded. "Okay, it all fits together. Except...whoever broke in probably used a key. Nathan gave Steve his key when he quit."

"He might have made an extra key, like Steve

said," suggested Violet.

The children thought about this for a moment.

"But why would Nathan steal things from Steve and Dawn?" asked Henry. "They helped him learn to be a baker. They even wanted him to take over Delilah's when they retired."

"Let's not rule him out yet," said Jessie. She looked over her notes. "The next person on my list is Charlie, the delivery man."

"He isn't very nice," said Benny.

"And he has a key to the shop," said Jessie.

"That's right," said Violet. "But Steve and Dawn say that Charlie wouldn't do anything to hurt the shop. They've known Charlie for a long time. If they trust him, we should too."

"Maybe," said Henry. "But remember how he knew about the break-in the same morning that it happened? And then there was that potato sack. Why would Charlie put it into his van instead of throwing it away?"

"It does seem like an odd thing to do," said Violet. "Maybe he decided to save it to carry things." She finished up her sandwich.

Suspects

Benny stopped running again. "All this thinking makes me hungry," he said. "I'm ready for dessert."

"Not just yet, Benny," Jessie said. "I have one more person on my list."

"Who could that be?" asked Violet. "I can't think of anyone else."

"It's Hilda Ramirez," Jessie said. "She seems really nice. Still, she might have been tempted to copy ideas that belonged to Delilah's."

"Charlie did say she was talking about the break-in after it happened," said Henry.

"I don't think it could be her," said Violet. "Hilda and Dawn are friends. They taught each other things. Hilda wouldn't do anything sneaky like that."

"But why are all those doughnut names almost the same?" asked Benny.

Henry shrugged. "Maybe Hilda *is* the person who stole the recipes, and she didn't think anyone would notice."

"*We* noticed," said Violet.

Henry stood up. "We don't know enough to solve this mystery yet," he said. "We can't prove that anyone stole the recipes. Officer Washington told us that we would need proof that there were written recipes to show they had been taken."

"That's true," said Jessie. "Is it possible that the recipes exist on paper somewhere?"

"Steve says they don't," said Violet.

Jessie shut her notebook. "But what if Steve is wrong?" She stood up. "There might be a way to find out. Come on. We need to do some investigating."

***

The Aldens decided to go to the library. Jessie thought there might be information there that wasn't anywhere else.

"If there is any more we can find out about Delilah's, it could be in old newspaper stories," Jessie told the others.

"I don't see how we can learn anything about what's happening now," said Benny as they stepped inside the library. "There's only old stuff in here."

"You'll see, Benny," Jessie told him.

They went to the reference desk for help. The librarian, Ms. Hester, wore a big button that said "Please Interrupt Me."

Suspects

Benny read the button. "Wow, this is the only place I've ever been asked to be rude!"

Ms. Hester laughed. Then she listened to Jessie's questions. She showed the children how to find old newspapers in online sources that the library had.

"You can type in a subject search term here," Ms. Hester told them. She pointed to a spot on-screen. "That will give you all the articles that mention your subject."

"Let's look for Delilah's Doughnut Shop," said Henry.

Jessie keyed in the search terms *Delilah's Doughnut Shop*. But only a couple articles came up. Then she tried putting in just *Doughnuts*.

"That's better!" said Violet. "There are more articles, and some of them are old."

The children read the articles. They learned about women like Delilah, who had gone to faraway places to make doughnuts for American soldiers during wartime—to give a sense of home. They learned that all the good feelings about doughnuts during wartime made them even more popular back in the United States. That was when shops like Delilah's opened up across the country.

But there wasn't much information about Delilah's.

"Why don't we start over?" said Henry. "We could just type in *Delilah's*. Or *Delilah Berg*."

"How about *Fred Berg* and *Delilah Berg*?" asked Jessie.

"That's okay," said Henry. "I think you have to put a plus sign instead of *and* because it's a search term."

Jessie typed in *Fred Berg + Delilah Berg*.

Several articles came up. "I don't think we've seen these before," said Violet.

"Look!" said Benny when Jessie had opened up the first article. "Is that a menu in that photo? I think it has doughnut names on it."

The children read a menu written on a chalkboard that Fred Berg proudly displayed.

"I found The Twisty!" said Benny, pointing to the screen.

"And there's The Masher...and Special Soldier's Doughnuts," said Violet. "Just what Steve said. The old names from Delilah's are practically the same as the new ones from The Donut Dispensary!"

"That might be important evidence," said Henry. "We should get a copy of the article." Jessie asked Ms. Hester to help her print a copy.

The children kept searching. A few minutes later, they found another article that looked interesting. A reporter had written about his interview of Fred Berg, Steve's father. At the time of the article, Fred and Delilah still owned the shop.

"Listen to this," said Jessie. She read aloud:

Greenfield News Reporter: Mr. Berg, you and your wife have been in business here for years. You must have made up a lot of your own recipes by now.

Fred Berg: Yes! We've both come up with our own special ones. Customers are always eager to find out what new doughnut will be next.

Reporter: Maybe you'll write a cookbook some day!

The Doughnut Whodunit

Fred Berg: Oh no. We won't ever do that. We've decided just to keep our recipes in the family. My wife doesn't even write down her recipes. She's good at keeping them in her head.

Reporter: What about you? I'm aware you are in charge of some of the stranger inventions that Delilah's is known for. Do you write them down?

Fred Berg: Yes, to tell you the truth, I have to keep my crazy ideas on paper. Otherwise I won't be able to duplicate them. They're all in a little sugar tin that I call my Vault.

CHAPTER 7

A Night Prowler

The Aldens made a copy of the interview and left the library. They talked on their way back to the shop, where Grandfather would be picking them up. Long shadows on Main Street made the walk a bit strange. Benny tried jumping on his own giant shadow as the children talked.

Violet huddled into her jacket. "So, now we know that some of the recipes were written down!" she said. "It's funny that Steve didn't know his dad was keeping notes all those years."

Jessie nodded. "Steve didn't know about the sugar tin either," she said. "It's too bad the shop is closed for the day. I want to find out what Steve and Dawn think about this news."

"I hope they have some ideas about where the tin could be," said Henry.

Jessie tied her scarf on tight. "I hope so too," she said. "I knew people kept lots of food in metal tins a long time ago. But I have no clue what an old sugar tin looks like. For all we know, it's hidden in the shop somewhere. Come here, Benny. I'll tie your scarf."

"Thanks," said Benny. "I'm all shivery."

Though it was only early evening, it was starting to get dark. The streetlights of Greenfield blinked on. An evening breeze made the Aldens walk fast.

"Why is there a light in Delilah's?" asked Benny. "You said it was closed."

The other Aldens looked. The front of the shop was very dark, but a light seemed to be on in the back room.

"Maybe Steve and Dawn are working late," said Jessie. "We can tell them about Fred's sugar tin."

Jessie tried the door and found that it was unlocked. The Aldens walked into the dark room. They could barely see the outlines of chairs and tables. The bells on the door jingled, startling everyone. Benny grabbed Violet's hand.

Sounds of movement came from the back. Jessie led the others forward quietly.

"Steve? Dawn?" Henry whispered. "We found some information..."

The sounds from the back room continued. The children crept closer to the kitchen door. Could it be Steve or Dawn—or was it someone else, someone who wasn't supposed to be there?

Jessie reached the doorway first and peered inside. She gasped. "What are you doing here?"

It was Nathan. He stood at the big center table in the kitchen. Mixing bowls, utensils, and ingredients were on the table. He went pale with surprise.

"Wow! You people scared me," he said. He put down the spoon he was holding and took a deep breath. "It's no big deal. I wasn't doing anything wrong."

The Aldens came into the kitchen.

"What do you mean?" asked Violet. "What are you doing back here?"

"You must be the person who's stealing Steve's recipes!" said Benny. "We caught you."

A Night Prowler

"Stealing recipes?" said Nathan.

Jessie explained about the copied doughnuts at the other doughnut shop. "We know someone's been making the exact same doughnuts as Delilah's."

"Well, it isn't me," said Nathan. "That's terrible. Why would anyone do that?" Nathan pounded the table with his fist. "I'd like to catch whoever stole those recipes myself."

"Then why are you here when the shop is closed?" asked Violet.

Nathan sat down on a stool. "Look," he said, "I know I don't work here. And I'm sorry I made you worry. It's just that no matter how hard I try, I can't remember how to make Steve's chocolate icing. I was trying to remember what to do."

"Were you looking for his secret recipe?" asked Jessie.

"It's not a secret recipe," said Nathan. "It's just a really good one. I wanted to remember it. I tried to make it at The Donut Dispensary, but my mind went blank every time. I thought if I made the icing in this kitchen again, the recipe might come back to me."

"I guess that seems reasonable," said Henry. "But did you tell Steve or Dawn you were coming?"

Nathan shook his head. "I know it looks weird. But I just couldn't tell them. I didn't think they'd want me in their kitchen anymore."

"You must have an extra key," said Benny. "That means you did the break-in. Doesn't it?"

Again, Nathan shook his head. "The truth is that I just walked in tonight."

"It's all right," said Henry. "Steve told me he'd leave the door open so we wouldn't freeze before Grandfather came to pick us up."

"So...you're sure you don't know anything about any written recipes?" asked Jessie.

"There are written recipes?" said Nathan. "I can't believe it!" He shook his head again. "If I'd had those when I worked here, my job would have been a whole lot easier. I probably wouldn't have left!"

Nathan stood up. "I should clean up the kitchen and leave. Steve and Dawn won't be happy knowing that I was here. They're probably already mad at me for quitting the way I did."

"I don't think they're mad at you," said Jessie.

"But they're super busy right now. We're helping them out."

Nathan cleaned up. He was quiet while he worked.

After he left, the Aldens did too. They made sure the door was locked behind them. Then they sat on the bench in front of Delilah's to wait for Grandfather.

Grandfather arrived soon after that. The children were extra happy to be out of the chilly weather. As they rode home, they talked.

"I think Nathan's telling the truth," said Violet. "He was mad when he heard about the stolen recipes."

Henry nodded slowly. "I think you're right, Violet. And Nathan was so surprised when he heard about the recipes being written down. He really doesn't seem to know anything about that."

"But if Nathan's no longer a suspect," said Jessie, "there are only two more people on our list: Charlie and Hilda."

"That makes it easier, doesn't it?" asked Benny.

"I'm not so sure about that," said Jessie, closing her notebook.

CHAPTER
8

The Missing Tin

"We've been so busy this week," said Violet. "I hope we have time to help Steve and Dawn with redecorating."

The Aldens were walking down Main Street the next morning. It was warm and sunny again, and not too windy.

"I'm going to show them my photos of The Donut Dispensary," Violet continued. "I've got some good ideas for paint colors. And maybe some new signs too."

"We've got to find out who's causing all the problems," said Henry. "Then we can talk about redecorating."

"Maybe it will cheer up Dawn and Steve if they

have something else to think about," said Violet. "Something that's fun, like new colors."

"Maybe," said Jessie. "I really want to tell them about Nathan. And about the sugar tin. Steve might remember the tin and know where it is. Or where it *was*."

"Hey!" shouted Benny. "Did those guys change their sign again?"

Benny pointed to the sign in front of The Donut Dispensary. Someone had erased the name *Mashup* and written a new name: *Smashed Potato Donut*.

"Wow," said Henry. "Whoever copied that doughnut must have just figured out the name was too much like The Masher."

"That wasn't very smart of the copycat," said Violet. "They should have picked a different name before they advertised the doughnut, not after."

The children moved on, talking about the name change.

When they arrived at Delilah's, Steve was busy with customers. But Dawn greeted them.

"We have so much to tell you!" said Jessie. She

handed Dawn the articles they had copied in the library.

Dawn sat down and read the articles. "A sugar tin!" she said. "I had no idea. I don't think Steve did either. And all this time, Steve thought his parents both kept their recipes locked up in their own memories."

"Only Delilah had hers memorized. Not Fred," said Henry.

Dawn put down the articles. "You know...I think I do remember a fancy old metal tin on a shelf with other knickknacks out here in the front," she said. "I never thought of looking inside it. I just dusted it now and then. I always kept those decorative things the way Fred and Delilah had them."

"Let's see if it's still there," said Jessie.

"I can climb up and get it!" said Benny. He darted off toward the shelf of knickknacks.

"I don't think it's there anymore," said Dawn, getting up. "Wait, Benny!"

But Benny didn't wait. By the time Dawn and the other children got to him, Benny had dragged a chair over and was hanging onto the shelf.

The Missing Tin

"Come on, Benny," said Henry. "You might topple that whole shelf. With you under it!" Henry wrapped his arms around his little brother and lifted him away from the shelf.

"Is it up there?" asked Benny when he was down on the ground. "Is it?"

"No," said Dawn, sighing. "I remember now. It was one of the few things we couldn't find after the break-in. I suppose we could look around, though."

Dawn and the Aldens began searching everywhere in the back room and the storeroom. But there was no old sugar tin anywhere.

"What's this about a tin?" asked Steve from the doorway.

Jessie told Steve about the article.

"I am completely dumbfounded!" said Steve. "How could I have missed seeing my dad write down his recipes?"

"Your dad probably knew how good you were at memorizing," said Dawn. "I'll bet he didn't think you'd ever need the written recipes. So, he didn't think he had to show them to you."

"He kept them for himself," said Henry. "And

maybe for anyone else in your family who might need them."

Steve just nodded his head silently. He looked amazed.

"But the tin isn't here anymore," said Violet. "What can we do?"

"We can help our customers," said Dawn. "I think they're waiting for us." Dawn and Steve left to take care of business.

But Violet went back to the hallway to look at an old photo on the wall.

"What's going on?" Henry asked her.

"I've been thinking and thinking," said Violet. She walked out slowly with the photo in her hands. "Fred wrote down the recipes for himself and his family. You know, to pass on to a family member who might keep the doughnut shop."

"And here's a picture of his family," said Henry. "But we already know everyone in that picture."

"No, we don't," said Jessie. "Not really. What about Steve's little brother, that boy in the picture? He'd be grown up now."

"What if this grown-up brother knew about the

The Berg family, in front of Grandad's favorite hangout, Griffith's Doughnut Shop. Pictured: Fred and Ruthie Berg with their sons, Derek C. and Steven E.

written recipes?" said Violet. "What if he came here looking for them?"

"That would explain the break-in," said Henry. "The brother could have been looking for papers, even behind the photos on the walls."

"I think we're onto something," said Jessie, sitting down at an empty table. "I wonder if it's important that Steve seemed so uncomfortable when we asked him about his brother."

"It might be," said Henry. He sat down next to Jessie and took the family photo from Violet.

"Fred's brother is Dave C. Berg," he said. "We don't know anyone named Dave Berg."

"And we have only two people left on our list of suspects," said Jessie. "Charlie, the delivery man, and Hilda."

Benny came over and looked at the photo too. "Charlie starts with a C," he said. "I see a big C there." Benny pointed at the caption under the picture.

Henry's eyes got big. "Could the C stand for *Charlie*?"

"What if it *is* Charlie?" said Jessie. "What if Charlie is Fred's brother?"

"Charlie the delivery man looks like Fred a little," said Benny, jumping up and down. "They're both really tall and skinny."

"But how come Fred never told us?" asked Violet. "Why would something like that be a secret?"

"Let's see if we can find out right now," said Henry. The Aldens went to the front of the shop.

***

Steve couldn't stop to talk to the Aldens until the morning rush was over. But then he sat down with them.

"We've been wondering if Charlie is your brother," Jessie told him. "We think he might be."

"Wow," said Steve. "How on Earth did you figure that out?"

Violet held up the old photo. "We put the pieces together. We weren't sure about it, which is why we're asking you," she said.

"You kids aren't just hard workers," said Steve. "You're smart!" He sighed. "Yes, Charlie's my brother. He's the boy in that photo."

"But why were you keeping that a secret?" asked Violet.

The Doughnut Whodunit

Steve looked serious. "That's another story, I'm afraid. It's not as happy as the first one I told you." Steve continued: "My brother left Greenfield a long time ago, when he was quite young. He didn't want to be part of my parents' business. He went to New York to make a name for himself. He wanted to become a success all on his own, without any help from his family."

"*Did* he become a success?" asked Jessie.

"Yes, as a matter of fact, he did," said Steve. "He became well known as a businessman. But it didn't last forever. Last year, Dave—or Charlie, as you know him—his business failed. Everyone knew about it. It was on the news for weeks."

"Poor Dave," said Benny. "I wouldn't want to be known for something that didn't work."

Steve nodded. "I think Dave was really ashamed about how things turned out. About six months ago, he called me. He told me he wanted to come back to Greenfield to live, but he needed some favors from me."

"Did he want to make doughnuts after all?" asked Benny.

The Missing Tin

"The favors he asked me for didn't have anything to do with doughnuts," said Steve. "Dave asked me to help him find a job in Greenfield. I have friends who own the local delivery service, so I made a phone call and recommended Dave. And that's how he got the job he has."

"But Dave asked for other favors, right?" said Henry.

Steve nodded. "He asked Dawn and me to promise not to tell anyone that he was the famous Dave Berg who had failed at his business. No one was supposed to know he was my brother. When he came back to Greenfield, he started using his middle name. He became Charlie Berg, not Dave Berg."

The Aldens sat, thinking about this. "Wouldn't people recognize him from before he left town?" asked Jessie.

"Probably not," said Steve. "After Dave left for college, he almost never came back to visit. People change a lot in thirty years."

"Do you think Charlie—er...Dave could have known about the sugar tin and the recipes?" asked Henry.

"I suppose he might have," said Steve. "He was my dad's favorite son, after all. And I was my mom's favorite. I spent more time cooking with my mom, and Dave cooked mostly with my dad."

"It sounds like Dave enjoyed making doughnuts as much as you do," said Violet. "I wonder why he didn't want to join you in the doughnut business."

Steve stared out the window. "Dave and I didn't always get along," he said. "Before he left for college, he was always trying to compete with me. But we were so far apart in age that he really couldn't ever be the winner. That might be why he felt he had to leave Greenfield. I missed my brother after he left."

"You told us you and Dawn really trust your brother," said Jessie. "But he might have taken those recipes."

"I still trust him," said Steve. "I don't believe he would have stolen anything from me. And I don't believe he would have lied either."

"But *someone* took the recipes," said Henry. "And someone is using them to make copies of your doughnuts."

The Written Proof

After the morning rush, the Aldens met again on the bench.

"Now we know there were written recipes," said Jessie. "But we still don't know who has the tin. Somehow, we'll have to find it."

"We all looked so carefully in Delilah's," Violet pointed out. "I don't think it's there."

"I've been thinking about that," said Henry. "Because the copycat doughnuts came from The Donut Dispensary, that should be where we look next."

Violet nodded. "It seems like the right idea," she said.

The Aldens passed the Greenfield Police Station

on their way to The Donut Dispensary. Officer Washington was just coming down the stone steps on her way out.

"Hello there!" she said. "How are things going?"

Jessie showed the officer the article that mentioned the sugar tin.

"You children did some good hunting," said Officer Washington. "I'd consider this proof that there were written recipes. On the other hand, you don't know for sure that they still exist—or where they might be."

"Will you come with us to The Donut Dispensary?" asked Henry. "We were just going to check on an idea we had."

"I can do that," she said. "I'm on my lunch break and can head over with you right now."

When the children and Officer Washington got inside the crowded shop, they walked toward the back.

"Excuse me," said Officer Washington to someone in the kitchen. The Aldens came to the doorway. What they saw surprised them all.

Hilda and Charlie stood at a counter in the small

kitchen. In front of them was a simple metal box. It was about as big as a loaf of bread. Pieces of paper with handwriting on them were spread out on the counter. The paper was yellowed and curled.

Charlie took a step away from the counter when he saw the Aldens and Officer Washington. "What's going on?" he said. "Why are you all here?"

"Is something the matter, Officer?" asked Hilda. "Why are these children here?"

"We think something wrong is going on in this shop," said Henry. "That's why we brought Officer Washington with us. Jessie, show Hilda the newspaper clippings."

Jessie handed the articles to Hilda.

"Is that the sugar tin Steve's dad kept?" asked Benny, pointing to the metal box.

"How do you know about this tin?" asked Charlie. He sounded angry.

"You can read the article too," said Jessie. "It tells about all the recipes your father wrote down. We've been looking for that tin."

"And now we found it," said Violet.

"I'm the owner here," said Hilda. She shook

hands with Officer Washington and introduced herself. "I'm confused. What's this about the recipes? Why are they so important? And why do the police need to be involved?"

Officer Washington explained, "I'm just here to help everyone sort this out. The Aldens have been investigating quite the mystery."

The Written Proof

"Steve always kept the family recipes secret," said Henry. "He didn't want anyone else knowing how to make his dad's doughnuts."

Jessie continued. "Steve never knew that his dad wrote down the recipes. Then doughnuts that looked and tasted like his dad's appeared at The Donut Dispensary. No one could figure out how it happened."

"Until we found the article," said Violet. "Then we knew that someone had probably stolen the tin and was copying the doughnuts—in this very shop."

"They even stole the names of the doughnuts— almost!" said Benny.

Officer Washington shifted from one foot to the other. "Ms. Ramirez, can you tell us anything about people making copied doughnuts in your shop?"

Hilda held out her hands and shrugged. "Charlie shared these recipes with me," she said. "I assumed they were his old recipes. We've made quite a few test batches. We're working together on them. We were planning to add a lot of new doughnuts to the menu."

"What do you have to say about this?" Officer

Washington asked Charlie.

Charlie carefully picked up the paper recipes and put them in the metal tin. He placed the cover on the tin and held it out to Officer Washington.

"It was me," he said. He looked down at his feet. "I knew the recipes were somewhere at Delilah's, so I went and found them."

"But why?" asked Violet. "You could have made those doughnuts with Steve."

"I didn't want people to know I am Steve's brother," said Charlie sadly. "I didn't want them to know my business had failed and I had come back to town. I thought if I worked with him, people would start to wonder. Plus, Steve and Dawn like to make classic doughnuts. I don't think they'd want to work with me."

Charlie sighed and went on. "When I first came back to town, I was glad about the new doughnut shop. Later on, I discovered that Hilda wanted to experiment with new ideas too. And I wanted to work with someone who'd be willing to do that. For the first time, I could see a fresh start for myself. I would carry on my father's doughnut tradition."

"We decided to start with the recipes from the tin and then see what we might want to do next," said Hilda. "I'm sorry."

"Hilda hired me to help her," said Charlie. "She didn't know the recipes were family secrets. I never thought anyone would realize we were using those old recipes. That's why I didn't try to hide their names. Then later, I saw all of you comparing The Twisters and The Twisties. I knew you were suspicious. I asked Hilda to change the name of The Mashups."

Charlie looked up at Hilda. Then he looked at Officer Washington. "Maybe I won't be working for anyone now. Maybe I'm in trouble."

"Why did you take that empty potato sack from Delilah's?" said Henry. "Was that part of trying to copy old recipes too?"

Charlie nodded. "I remembered the potato doughnut recipe for the most part, but I couldn't think of what kind of potato my dad used. I also needed to see The Mashers and taste them to make sure I'd made them correctly. It's a pretty tricky recipe to get right."

"That's why you broke into the shop, isn't it?" asked Violet. "You had to get some Mashers."

"Not exactly," said Charlie. He looked very unhappy. "I came looking for the recipes. I thought they might even be hidden behind those photos that have been on the wall for so long. I looked everywhere. Then I saw the old tin. And when I saw The Mashers, I had to take them. I knew they would help me recreate my dad's recipe."

Officer Washington held on to the sugar tin. "I'm going to take this tin back to Delilah's now," she said. "I will talk with Dawn and Steve about how they would like to handle this. In the meantime, Ms. Ramirez, please remove all of Charlie's recipes from your menu."

"Of course, Officer," said Hilda. "Please tell them I'm sorry this has happened."

"Officer," said Charlie, "I'd like to come with you and the children to Delilah's. I think maybe it's time for me to talk to my brother, fair and square."

***

Back at Delilah's, Steve sat down with Charlie at a corner table. Steve held the sugar tin on his lap.

The Written Proof

Officer Washington and the Aldens waited across the room. After a while, the two brothers stood up and shook hands.

"Are they friends now?" asked Benny. "Brothers are supposed to be friends, aren't they?"

"Yes," said Jessie. "Brothers should be friends. But I'm not sure if those brothers will be." Jessie glanced over at the men, who were still talking.

After another minute, Steve and Charlie walked toward the Aldens and Officer Washington. Charlie looked relieved. Steve still held the sugar tin.

"I won't be taking this matter any further, Melinda," Steve said. "Charlie and I have an agreement now. We're going to see how things go for a while."

Charlie smiled nervously. "We're going to try working together," he said.

"Cool!" said Benny. "You'll probably make even more crazy doughnuts than ever."

"Maybe," said Steve. "We have to see."

Charlie said, "We realized that we both wanted the same thing: to continue our parents' ways of making and selling doughnuts. I'd always thought

Steve wouldn't agree to try anything new or unusual, like our dad used to do. He seemed to want to make only our mother's recipes. But I guess I was wrong."

Steve smiled a little. "I was wrong too," he said. "I shouldn't have been so stubborn about wanting to stick to the old-fashioned doughnuts. I hardly ever made the newer recipes Dad made up—even the really good ones."

"So," said Charlie, "we're going to see if we can keep on remembering that we have the same goals: to keep making customers feeling welcome at Delilah's."

"And, if Charlie and I can meet each other halfway," said Steve, "then he can work for Delilah's. And try new ideas here too."

"That sounds like a fine plan," said Officer Washington. "I don't think I'm needed here any longer. But I'll take my usual cup of coffee to go."

"Coming right up," said Dawn, who had joined the group.

"I think we'd better get our aprons back on," said Violet. "It's almost time for the afternoon crowd to come."

The Written Proof

"Sure," said Steve. "But first, I'm putting this tin away, where only *we* can find it!" He patted Charlie on the back, and both of them smiled.

CHAPTER
10

A New, Old Shop

Two weeks later, on a Saturday, there was great excitement at the Alden home. The whole family was going to town for a special event. Violet was extra eager to get to Greenfield.

Grandfather smiled down at her. "I know you didn't do every bit of the plan," he said. "But you did come up with the best ideas. I'm very proud of you."

Violet beamed. She'd brushed her hair and checked her outfit in the mirror more than once. She was wearing jeans and her favorite purple sweater. "We haven't seen the finished product," she told her grandfather. "I'm super excited to see how everything looks all together."

Benny came hopping down the stairs to the

front hallway. "Where are our aprons?" he asked. "We have to have them. And they have to be clean and neat!"

Henry and Jessie laughed as they came down the stairs behind Benny. "This might be the first time I've heard Benny insist on something being clean and neat," said Jessie.

"Well, they *are* important items for the celebration, after all," said Henry.

"Don't worry, Benny," said Jessie. "I have the aprons in my backpack. They've been washed and ironed."

Benny looked relieved. "I sure wouldn't want to look messy," he said. Everyone laughed. Benny had never minded looking messy before.

As the Aldens drove to Greenfield, Benny said, "There's a big surprise just for us—Dawn said so!" He bounced up and down in his seat.

"We know, Benny," said Henry. "She also said we'd be surprised to see who's working at Delilah's now."

"I just can't wait to see how all of our ideas turned out," said Violet. "It was kind of hard to go back to school this week. I kept thinking about what the final touches would look like."

"I wonder what kind of party there's going to be," said Jessie. "It's nice and warm today, so I think it will be outside."

"I know something about it," said Benny.

"What's that?" asked Jessie.

"There will be plenty of...doughnuts!" Benny sang as he bounced. "Surprises and doughnuts! Surprises and doughnuts! We all love surprises and doughnuts!"

Grandfather and the children laughed.

Mr. Alden parked the car around the corner from Delilah's. Benny wanted to race ahead, but Mr. Alden turned to talk to the children.

"This is a big day for all of you," he told them. "Not only did you help redecorate Delilah's, but you solved an important mystery for the shop. You've made some people very happy. You helped bring two brothers together too." He hugged each of his grandchildren.

"And now, let's celebrate!"

The Aldens could hear the sounds of people

laughing and talking before they came around the corner. The first thing they saw, though, were the balloons. Blue, green, and white balloons were tied with ribbon to the newly painted bench out front, to new planters on either side of the bench, to the front door, and even to the waste bin and the streetlight in front of Delilah's.

Children marched around, eating doughnuts and wearing blue and green party hats. Adults chatted, sipped coffee, and nibbled on doughnuts. Everyone seemed to be smiling.

"I see Officer Washington!" cried Benny. He waved to her.

"Congratulations," said the officer. She came over and introduced herself to Mr. Alden. "This is a good day to celebrate the beautiful new shop," she said. "I hear you children had a lot to do with that."

"We just did some of the painting last weekend," said Henry. "And we gave Dawn and Steve some ideas. They did the rest."

"It's not really a *new* shop, is it?" asked Jessie. "At least, I hope it hasn't changed too much."

"Go and see," said Officer Washington. "I won't

hold you up."

The Aldens went into Delilah's.

"It's so much brighter!" said Violet. "Look! The pictures are up again."

Delilah's had had a makeover: Gone was the flowered wallpaper. In its place were two cream-colored walls and two bright blue walls. Along the edges of the walls was a stripe of pale green trim. The posters and photos looked wonderful against the newly painted walls.

Gone too were the curtains. The windows were bright and shiny; sleek blinds were there to keep the sun out when needed. The wooden trim and the counter had all been sanded and polished smooth. From the ceiling hung bright globe-shaped light fixtures.

"Aldens!" called Dawn. She was wearing a blue apron now. It was the same shade as the walls and the same shade as the aprons the Alden children had.

"What do you think of our shop now?" asked Dawn.

"It's great," said Jessie. "I love the matching aprons. Does Steve have a blue one too?"

A New, Old Shop

Dawn nodded. Steve, wearing his blue apron, was just coming out from the kitchen with a new tray of doughnuts. And right behind him came two more people, also wearing blue aprons.

"Nathan!" called Jessie.

"And Charlie too," said Henry.

Charlie smiled as he approached. "I never did get used to people calling me that name. I've decided I like going by Dave better."

"But aren't you afraid people will know about your old business?" Benny whispered.

"Oh, that's old news. I've got a new business I'm proud to be a part of." Dave put his hand on his brother's shoulder.

"And now we've got all the help we could need," said Steve. "I lured Nathan back to Delilah's too."

Nathan blushed a little. "It was easy. Steve's going to let me keep a notebook while I'm learning. No more sneaking in at night to practice."

"You all look like a team now," said Jessie. "We should put on our aprons too." Jessie pulled the children's aprons from her bag and handed them to her siblings.

"We'd make a great picture," said Dawn, looking around at all of Delilah's workers.

"A real photo opportunity!" said Violet, holding up her camera. "Why don't we go outside? We could stand under the new sign. We didn't get a good look at it when we got here."

"Not yet," said Steve. "You haven't gotten your big surprise, Aldens."

Steve made the children wait at one of the tables. He went back to the kitchen and came out with a baking tray.

"Presenting The Alden!" said Steve, putting the tray down in front Benny, whose eyes grew. On the tray were rectangular doughnuts covered with pale green icing and blue and white sprinkles.

"You children get the first taste," said Dawn.

Violet took a picture of the tray first. "They match the new decor!" she said. "Everyone should get the first taste!"

Benny, Violet, Jessie, and Henry each took a doughnut. Then Grandfather, Steve, Dawn, Dave, and Nathan took theirs. There was quiet munching for a few seconds.

The Doughnut Whodunit

"Mmmm!" said Benny. "I'm glad there are more! These are amazing!"

"There's something special in this doughnut," said Henry. "I don't know what it is."

"We can't tell you!" said Nathan. "It's a secret ingredient. But if you keep tasting, you might figure it out yourself."

Everyone laughed.

"Can we take our picture now?" asked Violet.

"Sure," said Steve. "In fact, I think the *Greenfield News* team has arrived. They can take our picture for the paper."

"Wow," said Benny. "We'll be famous."

Back outside, the first person to greet Delilah's team was Hilda Ramirez. She hugged Dawn and shook hands with everyone. "You folks look great. And the shop does too! I really love your sign."

The children stepped back from the door. Above it was a big new sign, made out of polished wood and shiny metal.

"'Delilah's Doughnut Shop,'" read Benny.

A man with a camera came up to the group. "Are these all the helpers?"

A New, Old Shop

"They sure are," said Steve.

"Well, everyone, face me, and we'll take some photos for the paper. Say *apple fritter*!"

***

When the party was over, Steve and Dawn let the Aldens take home the rest of their special doughnuts. There would be more batches coming soon to Delilah's.

In the car, Benny looked into the paper bag of doughnuts. He'd promised to wait till after dinner to have his.

"Why are you looking so hard at those doughnuts?" asked Violet. "I can't believe you want to eat more already. Do you?"

"I'm thinking," said Benny. "These doughnuts are the same shape as a boxcar!"

"That's true," said Violet slowly. She looked into the bag Benny was holding. "I'm getting ideas for redecorating our clubhouse. Thanks, Benny!"

"You're welcome," said Benny. "Doughnuts make everyone think better, don't they?"

Turn the page to read
a sneak preview of

THE ROBOT
RANSOM

**the next
Boxcar Children mystery!**

Benny Alden knelt on the floor of the boxcar, nose to nose with a one-foot-tall robot. "Hi, DogBot!" he said.

"*Arf!*" The robot barked and rolled back and forth on its wheels.

Six-year-old Benny laughed. "I see why you call it DogBot. It doesn't look like a dog, but it barks like one!"

His brother Henry grinned. "We modeled the robot after a search and rescue dog. The barking is just for fun." At fourteen, Henry was the oldest of the Alden siblings.

Twelve-year-old Jessie nodded. "Search and rescue dogs affected our design. But our robot doesn't have to look like a real dog."

The robot backed away from Benny and began exploring the room. When DogBot got to a wall, it turned. Soon the robot dog got close to the Aldens' real dog, a wire fox terrier named Watch. DogBot let out another friendly *"Arf!"* Watch just backed into a corner and growled.

Violet, who was ten, hurried to give Watch a hug. "Don't worry. We would never replace you with a robot dog!" Watch licked her face and then turned to look suspiciously at DogBot. The children laughed.

Henry checked the time on his phone. "Is everyone ready to leave?"

"Our suitcases are in the house," said Violet. "I helped Benny pack."

"All right," said Henry, picking up DogBot. "Say good-bye to the boxcar for a few days."

"We'll have to say good-bye to Watch too." Violet gave the dog another hug. "We'll miss you, but you wouldn't like being around all those robots."

"Thousands and thousands of robots!" said Benny. "I can't wait."

"Well, hundreds of robots anyway." Henry led the way back to the house. "This is a regional Robot Roundup. We're one of ten middle school teams competing."

"That sounds like a tough contest," said Violet.

Benny skipped ahead toward the house and called back, "Henry and Jessie can win."

Henry smiled. "Thanks. Winning would be nice. But no matter what happens, we've already learned a lot in robotics club."

"It has been fun," said Jessie. "We're lucky that our team members have so much experience." As the children went through the back door of the house, the front doorbell rang. "That must be Naomi and Rico now!"

The Aldens hurried to answer the door, where Jessie introduced her teammates to Violet and Benny. "Naomi and Rico have done this competition for two years," she said.

Naomi had dark skin and a puffy halo of black hair. She said, "Each team has four students. Our old teammates are in high school this year. We sure are glad Henry and Jessie joined us."

Rico was tall, with tan skin and dark hair falling into his eyes. "We need a good team if we're going to beat Silver City." Watch came up and sniffed at Rico's knee, making him jump. Then he bent down to pet the dog.

"The Greenfield STEAM Team can do it!" said Naomi.

Violet was often shy with strangers, but Naomi was wearing a purple shirt. Purple was Violet's favorite color. She immediately liked the older girl, so she said, "That's a good team name. I'm glad you included Art along with Science, Technology, Engineering, and Math. I like STEAM better than STEM."

"Oh, I get it now," said Benny. "STEAM comes from the first letters of those other words."

"That's right, Benny," Jessie said proudly. Then she turned to Naomi. "Violet is an artist."

"That's great," Naomi said. "Art is an important part of science and engineering. Maybe you'll join the robotics club in a couple of years."

Grandfather entered the room. Henry introduced him to Naomi and Rico. "Thank you for offering to drive us," said Rico.

Grandfather nodded. "I have business near

Port Elizabeth. We'll stay at the hotel together. I can drop you off and then take care of my work. It will be fun for Violet and Benny to see all the robots too. Shall we go?"

Once they were on the road, Violet turned to Rico. "You said you want to beat the Silver City team. What about the other teams?"

"Sure," said Rico. "But the Greenfield STEAM Team and the Silver City Gearheads are rivals."

"Tell them what happened last year," said Henry.

Rico nodded. "The Silver City team is very competitive, especially this boy named Logan. He can get pretty insulting."

"He doesn't have the right spirit for the Robot Roundup," Naomi said. "But that's not the worst part. Last year, we won fair and square, but Logan complained. He said the judges hadn't given us the right score."

Violet stared at her with wide eyes. "What happened?"

Naomi shrugged. "The judges stayed with

their decision. We got the trophy and the prize money. But Logan and the Gearheads kept saying bad things about us. It took some of the fun out of winning."

Jessie made a face. "I'm not looking forward to meeting him."

When they arrived at the hotel, everyone grabbed their luggage and piled out. They carried their things into the lobby and waited while Grandfather checked in.

Jessie looked around the lobby. "It's time to meet Coach Kaleka, but I don't see him yet."

Henry, Rico, and Naomi also looked around the lobby. A few people sat in chairs, while others came and went. Naomi said, "I don't see Coach. But there's the Silver City team!"

A short woman with big glasses was talking to four children. One of them, a boy about Henry's age, glanced around the room. When he spotted their group by the check-in desk, he walked over. "Look, it's the Greenfield *daydream* team," he said. "Because you're dreaming if you think you can beat us."

Naomi rolled her eyes. "Hello, Logan."

"Are these your new team members?" Logan pointed at Violet and Benny. "I guess even little kids could do better than you."

"Hey, I could make a good robot!" Benny said.

Henry stepped forward. "I'm Henry and this is my sister Jessie. We're the new members of the Greenfield STEAM Team. We're looking forward to a fun, fair competition with good sportsmanship."

Logan snickered at that. Before he could speak, Grandfather turned from the desk and handed the children keys. "Here you are, rooms two twenty-two and two twenty-four. Let's go unpack."

"What about Coach?" Naomi asked. "Should we wait for him?"

Henry asked the hotel clerk, "Has Mr. Kaleka checked in yet?" He spelled the name for her.

The woman checked the computer. "No one by that name has a reservation this weekend, and the hotel is all booked up. Lots of people are coming for the Robot Roundup."

"Thank you," said Henry, turning back to his family and teammates. "That's strange. But maybe Coach is staying at a different hotel."

"I'll text him and let him know our room numbers," suggested Rico.

"Good plan," said Grandfather. "Let's go to our rooms so we're not in the way here."

They grabbed their bags and headed down the hallway. Henry glanced back, but Logan had disappeared. So had his teammates and coach.

At their rooms, Henry pushed open the door that said 222. Something made a soft scuffling sound.

"What was that noise?" asked Rico.

Henry stepped into the room. "There's a piece of paper on the floor. The door pushed it back." He picked up the white paper. Words were written on it in black marker.

Greenfield, Go Home!

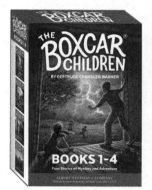
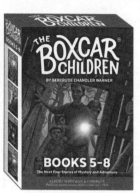
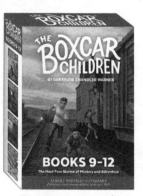

The Boxcar Children 20-Book Set includes Gertrude
Chandler Warner's original nineteen books,
plus an all-new activity book, stickers,
and a magnifying glass!

978-0-8075-0847-3 · US $132.81

THE BOXCAR CHILDREN

GREAT ADVENTURE

An Exciting 5-Book Miniseries

**Henry, Jessie, Violet, and Benny Alden
are on a secret mission that takes
them around the world!**

When Violet finds a turtle statue that nobody's seen
before in an old trunk at home, the children are on the
case! The clue turns out to be an invitation to the
Reddimus Society, a secret guild dedicated to returning
lost treasures to where they belong.

Now the Aldens must take the statue and six mysterious
boxes across the country to deliver them safely—and keep
them out of the hands of the Reddimus Society's enemies.
It's just the beginning of
the Boxcar Children's
most amazing
adventure yet!

JOURNEY ON A RUNAWAY TRAIN
Created by Gertrude Chandler Warner

HC 978-0-8075-0695-0
PB 978-0-8075-0696-7

THE CLUE IN THE PAPYRUS SCROLL
Created by Gertrude Chandler Warner

HC 978-0-8075-0698-1
PB 978-0-8075-0699-8

THE DETOUR OF THE ELEPHANTS
Created by Gertrude Chandler Warner

HC 978-0 8075-0684-4
PB 978-0-8075-0685-1

THE SHACKLETON SABOTAGE
Created by Gertrude Chandler Warner

HC 978-0-8075-0687-5
PB 978-0-8075-0688-2

THE KHIPU AND THE FINAL KEY
Created by Gertrude Chandler Warner

HC 978-0-8075-0681-3
PB 978-0-8075-0682-0

THE COMPLETE FIVE-BOOK MINISERIES
Created by Gertrude Chandler Warner

Also available as a boxed set!
978-0-8075-0693-6 · $34.95

Hardcover US $12.99 · Paperback US $6.99

GERTRUDE CHANDLER WARNER discovered when she was teaching that many readers who like an exciting story could find no books that were both easy and fun to read. She decided to try to meet this need, and her first book, *The Boxcar Children*, quickly proved she had succeeded.

Miss Warner drew on her own experiences to write the mystery. As a child she spent hours watching trains go by on the tracks opposite her family home. She often dreamed about what it would be like to set up housekeeping in a caboose or freight car—the situation the Alden children find themselves in.

While the mystery element is central to each of Miss Warner's books, she never thought of them as strictly juvenile mysteries. She liked to stress the Aldens' independence and resourcefulness and their solid New England devotion to using up and making do. The Aldens go about most of their adventures with as little adult supervision as possible— something else that delights young readers.

Miss Warner lived in Putnam, Connecticut, until her death in 1979. During her lifetime, she received hundreds of letters from girls and boys telling her how much they liked her books.